W9-AJS-080

To my sister Jennifer

First edition 2006

Library of Congress Cataloging-in-Publication Data is available.

Library of Congress Catalog Card Number 2005050184

ISBN 0-7636-2391-1

2 4 6 8 10 9 7 5 3 1

Printed in China

This book was typeset in Cochin.
The illustrations were done in pastel,
colored pencil, and gouache.

Candlewick Press
2067 Massachusetts Avenue
Cambridge, Massachusetts 02140

visit us at www.candlewick.com

Nell's Elf

Jane Cowen-Fletcher

CANDLEWICK PRESS
CAMBRIDGE, MASSACHUSETTS

It was raining, it was pouring, and Nell

had no one to play with and nothing to do.

She drooped.

She moped.

She sang,

"It's raining, its pouring, this dumb day is boring."

She sighed.

"I *need* someone to play with!" she said.

"If I had a sister or a brother

or a dog

or a cat

or even a mouse, I'd never be bored!"

She sighed again, then smiled.

"Or if I had an *elf* for a friend—my own elf—
I would never, ever be bored.

"He would be small," she said, "with pointy ears
and fluffy hair.

"He'd be wearing polka dots . . .

and stars . . .

and a rainbow . . .

and curly-toed shoes . . .

and a pointy hat with a feather!"
"No feather!" roared a small, elf-size voice.

And there he was!

"My elf!" cried Nell.

"*That's me!*"
said he.

He was perfect!

(Except for the feather.)

"So, you're bored, huh?" he said.

"There is no excuse for being bored."

"But it's raining," said Nell.

"So have . . . a PARTY!"

"A party?" asked Nell. "But—"

"First we'll need some chocolate chips," said the elf.

"What kind of party will this be?" asked Nell.

"The best kind," said the elf.

"AN ELF PARTY!"

"All we need are a few more guests!" the elf said.

So Nell invited them . . .

and they all came.

"Let the party begin!"

cried the elf.

What a party it was!

They sang elf songs.

They danced elf dances.

And they ate chocolate chips right out of the bag!

Since then, whenever it rains,

Nell invites her elf to come out and play.

And she is never, ever, *ever* bored.